THE UNDER DOGS

CATCH A
CAT BURGLAR

RAZORBILL

An imprint of
Penguin Random House LLC, New York

For our boys, Clancy and Arlo,
and their faithful hound. —KT & JT

For Mum and Dad. Thanks for all
the love and support. —SG

First published in Australia by Hardie Grant Children's Publishing in 2021
Published in the United States of America by Razorbill,
an imprint of Penguin Random House LLC, 2022
Text copyright © 2021 by Kate and Jol Temple
Illustration copyright © 2021 by Shiloh Gordon
Activities text copyright © 2022 by Penguin Random House LLC

Razorbill & colophon are registered
trademarks of Penguin Random House LLC.
Visit us online at penguinrandomhouse.com.

Library of Congress Cataloging-in-Publication Data
Names: Temple, Kate, author. | Temple, Jol, author. |
Gordon, Shiloh, illustrator.
Title: The Underdogs catch a cat burglar / Kate Temple,
Jol Temple ; art by Shiloh Gordon.
Description: New York : Razorbill, 2022. | Series: The
Underdogs ; book 1 | "First published in Australia by
Hardie Grant Children's Publishing in 2021." | Audience:
Ages 6-9 years. | Summary: The Underdog Detective
Agency has a proud tradition of sniffing out trouble,
but in order to catch Dogtown's elusive cat burglar, they
first enlist the help of a scruffy street cat named Fang.
Identifiers: LCCN 2022019099 | ISBN 9780593526965
(trade paperback) | ISBN 9780593526972 (ebook)
Subjects: CYAC: Dogs—Fiction. | Cats—Fiction. | Mystery
and detective stories. | Humorous stories. | LCGFT:
Detective and mystery fiction. | Humorous fiction.
Classification: LCC PZ7.T246 Un 2022 | DDC [Fic]—dc23
LC record available at https://lccn.loc.gov/2022019099

Printed in the United States of America

1st Printing

LSCH

Series design by Sarah Mitchell

The publisher does not have any control over and
does not assume any responsibility for author
or third-party websites or their content.

KATE AND JOL TEMPLE

THE UNDERDOGS

CATCH A CAT BURGLAR

ART BY
SHILOH
GORDON

RAZORBILL

CHAPTER 1

Let me tell you how many cats there used to be in
THE UNDERDOG DETECTIVE AGENCY...

Zero. Zilch. Not one.

Then along came **Fang**. One eye. Three teeth. A kink
in her tail. You wouldn't pick her as a **Dogtown**
detective, would you?

Hi there!

FANG:
· Tabby cat.
· Wants to be a detective.
· Loves sardines.

For starters, she's not a dog. She's a **cat**. Yes, yes, I know what you're thinking. What's a cat even doing in Dogtown? Well, there are **lots** of different animals living in Dogtown. True, it's mostly dogs, but there are **always** exceptions.

Fang is one of them.

WELCOME TO
DOGTOWN
PUPULATION: 1000000K-9

2

You see, Fang grew up in Dogtown. A **strange** place for a cat to grow up. But Fang's parents taught Cat at the local **school**, so Dogtown is all she ever knew.

At school, her dog friends showed her all the local customs.

How to **bark** at the door...

WOOF! WOOF!

BARK! BARK!

how to **chase** balls...

how to **whiz** on trees...

Step 1: Lift leg.
Step 2: Pee.

Fang's dog friends did all these things very well, and Fang did them all very **badly**.

Her bark was a **meow**...

BARK! BARK! BARK! MEEO

OWW! OOO

she got **bored** of chasing the same stupid ball...

When school finished, everyone went off to get jobs in Dogtown, including Fang.

She tried her **paw** as a sheep dog, but the sheep took no notice of her.

BAH!

She put up her **tail** to work in the ski resorts with the huskies, but she kept **falling** down.

She spent a week as a ball girl at the tennis club, but the Jack Russells just **shook** their heads.

EUGH!

She even tried out as an **Official Butt Sniffer**...

Her parents suggested she try something less **doggish**, like a curtain installer...

RIIIIIP!

But that didn't work out either. Fang knew there had to be **something** she was good at, but what?

What Fang needed was a **sign**.

DO YOU HAVE WHAT IT TAKES TO BE AN UNDERDOG DETECTIVE?

Hey, a sign!

Fang went inside. It didn't look much like a detective agency. It looked like a **soup factory**.

Wait a minute … IT **WAS** A SOUP FACTORY!

There was a conveyor belt with lots of cans going around on it, and a big bubbly pot of something that smelled **DISGUSTING!**

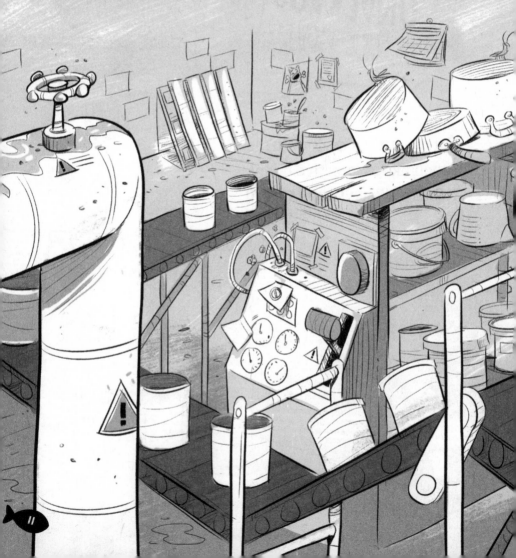

"Um, hello? Is this where I become a **dog detective**?" asked Fang.

A **gruff-looking** terrier answered her. "No. This is McTavish's Soup Factory. I'm Mrs. McTavish."

12

Fang crinkled her nose.

"What's that **TERRIBLE** smell?"

"That's my famous **brussels sprout** and **blue cheese** soup!" barked Mrs. McTavish. "If you're looking for the Underdog Detective Agency, it's upstairs."

She pointed to a **rickety** staircase, and Fang followed it upstairs. She was happy to get away from the **stench!**

"Hello?" called Fang. "Is **this** where I become a dog detective?"

CHAPTER 2

This is **Detective Barkley**. He's a German shepherd. Most German shepherds join the police force. Not Barkley. Sirens make him **howl**.

BARKLEY:
- German shepherd.
- Looks good in a trench coat.
- Bushy eyebrows.

BOSS DOG

"Okay, Carl, knock off the **gags**!" barked Detective Barkley. Barkley looked Fang up and down. "Are you delivering **fish heads**? The soup factory is **downstairs**."

"I'm not **delivering** anything," replied Fang. "I'm here about the job."

You are? You know this is a detective agency?

Sure.

"We're not some cat café." Barkley frowned. "We're detectives. We go **undercover** to investigate **mysteries** and solve **crimes**."

"That's what I want to do," said Fang.

Barkley raised one **bushy** eyebrow.

YOU want to go undercover to investigate mysteries and solve crimes?

YES, she did.

"What about **climbing**?"

"Better than a **monkey**."

"Got **sharp teeth**?"

"My name's **Fang**!"

"Okay, okay . . ." Barkley said. "But how do you feel about wearing a **disguise**? Cats hate **dressing up**."

Fang reached into her pocket. "I'm fine with it."

TA-DA!

Barkley couldn't quite put his paw on it, but he knew there was **something** he liked about Fang. And having a cat on the team might actually be a good idea. No one would ever suspect she was an **undercover DOG** detective.

"Have you ever heard of the cat burglar?" growled Barkley.

Everyone had heard of the cat burglar. Even Fang. The cat burglar had **stolen** everything in Dogtown, from **handbags** to **ham sandwiches**. Nobody had been able to catch him.

Barkley tapped his foot as he thought. *Why not use a cat to catch the cat burglar? It's so **absurd**, it just might work.*

"Congratulations, cat. I can't believe I'm saying this, but I'm giving you a **shot**. We need all the help we can get right now," said Barkley.

Fang grinned. "I can be very **PURRRRRR**suasive. When do I start?"

At that exact moment, the phone **rang**. Carl the Chihuahua receptionist looked at it in surprise.

AHH!

RING! RING!

"What's the **phone** doing?!" yelped Carl.

"Um, I think it's ringing," offered Fang helpfully.

"Oh, ringing!" said Carl. "That's right, I forgot phones did that."

"Well . . . Are you going to **answer** it?" asked Barkley.

Carl picked up the phone. "Hello? This is the . . . wait a minute . . . what are we called again?"

Barkley **grabbed** the phone from Carl. "Oh, for dog's sake! Hello, this is the Underdog Detective Agency, no clue left undug."

The voice on the other end of the phone was **LOUD.**

THE **CAT BURGLAR** HAS **STRUCK** AGAIN!

Barkley turned to Fang. "How about starting **right now**?"

CHAPTER 3

Fang couldn't believe it. She was an **UNDERDOG!**

As she looked around the **Underdog Detective Agency**, she could see there was another dog in the corner of the office. It wasn't hard to spot her, because she was covered in **spots**! It wasn't chicken pox or even dog pox... She was a Dalmatian.

"This is Dr. Spots. She's got a **gadget** for everything. Dr. Spots, this is Fang. Our new Underdog Detective," said Barkley.

DR. SPOTS:
- Dalmatian.
- Inventor of things that don't always work.

"That's a **brilliant** cat **costume**! I almost thought you were a cat," laughed Dr. Spots.

" ... I am a cat," said Fang.

Dr. Spots **gasped**. **"WHAAAAAT?"**

Barkley looked at her. "Fang is the **only** one who applied for the job, Spots! I'm sure she'll be all right once we show her the **ropes**."

"I **love** rope!" said Fang.

"There's no rope," grumbled Barkley. "It's just a saying."

"Oh, I knew that." This was **not true**. Fang didn't know the first thing about detective sayings or detective work.

Dr. Spots **shook** her head. "But..." she said.

No **buts**, and no **sniffing butts!** We all have to work together. But you only get one shot, Fang. Help us catch the cat burglar, or you're out on your tail.

The truth was, the Underdogs were **desperate**. They hadn't solved a case in years.

Well, that wasn't **exactly** true. They did solve the case of the **missing** sandwich (Carl ate it), the case of the **stolen** cupcake (Carl ate it), and the case of the **disappearing** sunglasses (they were on Carl's head).

These days, all the **BIG** cases went to the **Top Dog Detectives**. The Top Dogs were brother and sister Weimaraners who drove around town in their **flashy sports car** solving cases left, right, and center.

We're the best!

It's true!

THE TOP DOGS:
- Weimaraners. Brother-and-sister detective duo.
- Own lots of cool vehicles.

The more cases they solved, the more work they got, and the more **flashy** equipment they bought. They even had their own **helicopter**!

33

If the Underdogs could **crack** the cat burglar case, they just might be able to get back on top. And maybe get out of the **stinky** soup factory!

34

"Follow me," said Dr. Spots. "I've been working on something **high-tech** that will help us catch the cat burglar."

Barkley and Fang followed Dr. Spots down to the parking lot. Fang purred in **delight** when she saw the **shiny** new jeep parked down there.

"I've made a few **modifications** to the vehicle..." explained Dr. Spots.

"Let me guess," said Fang. "It's got a **laser-powered turbo-booster** for **maximum speed**?"

Dr. Spots just looked at Fang. "Not the jeep... That's Mrs. McTavish's. The bike." She pointed to a **rusty** old bike with **two** seats.

Fang tried not to look too disappointed. "So, what's the cool **gadget** then? Has it got **radar**? Or maybe a sonic **power-beam**?"

"I've added a **bicycle bell**," said Dr. Spots proudly.

"A bell?" said Fang. "Oh great. How can we catch the cat burglar with **that**?"

RING -A- LING!

"**Fussy**, are you?" grumbled Dr. Spots. "I've heard that about cats."

As Fang and Barkley got on the bike, a **text** came in on Barkley's cell phone. It was from Carl.

The cat burglar's just stolen a crate of sardines. Head to the fish markets.

Barkley and Fang rode **fast** toward the fish markets, dinging their bell. **DING! DING!** They were there in no time.

DING! DING!

Fang followed Barkley over to a market stall, where a **large pelican** was pacing back and forth. This wasn't any old pelican, mind you—it was **Max Pelicano**, the **boss** of the fish markets.

MAX PELICANO:
- Pelican.
- Fish market boss.
- Lover of seafood.

"What took you so long!" **squawked** Max. "And what'd you bring a cat here for? Don't you know they're **trouble**?"

"This is my new partner, Fang," explained Barkley.

"**Claw enforcement**," said Fang, sticking out a paw.

Max ignored it. "One of her kind has just cleaned me clear out of **sardines**! Every last one. It's that cat burglar, I tell you. I knew I should have called the Top Dog Detectives..."

"Forget about the Top Dogs, sir," said Barkley. "The Underdogs are **on the case**!"

Now, what makes you think it was the cat burglar?

FRESH COLLARMARI

Max Pelicano rolled his eyes. "Who else would **steal** a crate of the world's **finest** sardines?"

"Almost **everyone** likes sardines," said Fang. "Not just cats. Bears, seals, ducks. Even whales like sardines."

Max looked at Barkley, who just **shook** his head.

"Was this cat born yesterday? I think I'd know if a **WHALE** walked into my fish market!" spat Max Pelicano.

"Of **course** it was the cat burglar," said Barkley. "Look, there are **paw prints** everywhere. They sure don't belong to a whale!"

Fang wasn't so sure. Okay, maybe it wasn't a whale, but there was something **fishy** about those paw prints. See, while cats love sardines, they sure don't love **water**.

One thing was certain: Fang and Barkley needed more than a few wet splotches to solve this case. Luckily, Barkley knew **exactly** who to ask.

CHAPTER 4

"We should talk to Ratzak," said Barkley.

"Who's **Ratzak**?" asked Fang.

"He's a rat who lives under the pier," explained Barkley, hurrying back to the bike.

Barkley and Fang took off down a narrow lane that led to the pier. There they found an old **cardboard box** with the words **DO NOT DISTURB** scratched across it. Barkley knocked.

DO NOT DISTURB!

RATZAK
170613

RATZAK:
- Low-down dirty rat.
- A real snoop.
- Stinky.

"Can't you **read**?" shouted the rat, popping his angry head out. Ratzak was indeed a rat. Pointy **nose**. Sharp **teeth**. Cheese **breath**. Yep, he was a rat, all right, and he always knew **exactly** what was going down in Dogtown.

46

"Well, well, well, if it isn't Detective Barkley. I'd ask you in, but the place is a real **rat's nest**. Who's the cat?" he asked, looking at Fang suspiciously. Being a rat, Ratzak wasn't much of a cat person.

"She's the **newest** member of the Underdog Detective Agency," replied Barkley. "Meet Fang."

"An undercover **CAT?**" laughed Ratzak. "What's next? Firefighting sloths? So, what do you want to know?" he asked.

"In**FUR**mation. Do you know who stole the **sardines** from the fish market?" Fang asked.

"Maybe I saw something. Maybe I didn't. What's it worth to you?" said Ratzak.

It was worth exactly two and a half **cheese slices**, which Barkley carried on him at all times. Information didn't come cheap in Dogtown.

Ratzak **gobbled** up the cheese before replying. "All I know is this cat burglar can jump. I mean **REALLY** jump. I tried to get a good look, but that cat was gone in a **flash**. You've never seen anything like it!"

Fang had more **questions**, but just then another text message came in from Carl.

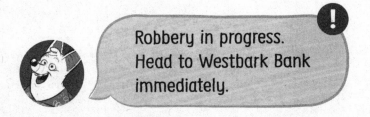

Robbery in progress. Head to Westbark Bank immediately.

"Two cases in one day?" Barkley scratched his head. "This **never** happens!"

They **jumped** on their rusty old bike and rode uphill to Uptown, where the **fancy** dogs lived.

They came to a **screeching** halt outside a big sandstone bank. Just then, a figure dressed in pink **leaped** from the second-story window onto a bright pink **electric scooter**!

"**WOW!**" exclaimed Fang. "That robber really **CAN** jump! Just like Ratzak said. It must be the cat burglar!"

"Follow that cat!" barked Barkley.

They set off in **hot pursuit**. Barkley sped up and down the streets of Dogtown, but as **fast** as he pedaled, the cat burglar was **faster**–darting down back alleys, over bridges and through tunnels.

LOST

CAT BURGLAR ON THE LOOSE

"This cat is **seriously** fast!" yelled Barkley as the cat began to get away.

Fang piped up. "Let's swap! I'll **steer**. I'm a cat, so I think like a cat!"

There was no time to argue. The cat burglar was getting away. Barkley jumped on the back seat and **pedaled** as **fast** as he could.

With a few **nimble** turns, they were back on the cat burglar's tail ... Well, not literally, because that would hurt.

"Good job, Fang! **Tail** that cat!" shouted Barkley.

"It already has a tail!" called Fang. "A **fluffy** black-and-white one!"

"It's a detective saying," sighed Barkley. "It means **follow** that cat!"

Fang and Barkley **swerved** and **darted** through the streets. With Fang steering and Barkley pedaling, they made a good team. They were close, but not so close that the cat burglar would notice them. It was good detective work.

But just at that moment, they passed the **squeaky toy** store.

Distracted by the noise, Fang swerved . . . and **crashed** right into a Starbark's Coffee Cart. Coffee went flying!

A confused beagle popped up from behind the **toppled** cart.

Did somebody order a puppycino?

The cat burglar had gotten away.

CHAPTER 5

Back above the soup factory, Dr. Spots was **not** impressed.

"At least it wasn't a **helicopter**," offered Fang hopefully.

"We don't have a helicopter. Only the Top Dogs have a helicopter. And now we don't even have a bike! So it's **walkies** for you…" Dr. Spots said.

It suited Fang to go for a walk, because Mrs. McTavish had just started cooking her next batch of soup—cabbage and octopus ink. **YUCK!**

With no **leads** (or **leashes**) on the whereabouts of the cat burglar, Fang and Barkley made their way back to the fish markets to **sniff** out some more clues.

"Sorry about crashing the bike, Barkley," said Fang nervously.

"Well, those **squeaky toys** are very distracting. And we're in this together now, so don't worry about it," said Barkley as they strolled along.

"So, I've been **wondering**—what makes a cat want to be an Underdog Detective anyway?"

Fang thought about it. "Purrrtecting **animals** is important, right?"

"Agreed," nodded Barkley.

"Besides," added Fang, "whatever a **dog** can do, a **cat** can do too."

You think so, do you?

Of course. I can speak Dog, for instance. I bet you can't speak Cat.

Barkley smiled, and then in fluent Cat said, "**Meeeow**."

Fang was **super** surprised. "You **DO** speak Cat!"

"Meeeooow meeeooooow!" said Barkley, which in Cat actually meant "I am a **turnip brain**". Fang was pretty sure this wasn't what Barkley meant, but it was a good try.

HA! HA! HA!

As they turned the corner, they came to a street that had been blocked off. A **crowd** of onlookers had gathered around a barrier.

"What's going on here?" Barkley asked.

"Could be a **clue**..." murmured Fang.

The crowd was **busy** taking photos. An excited turtle clutching a camera explained, "It's **Kitty DeClaw**! She's filming a TV ad for Meowy Chowy cat food!"

"Who?" asked Barkley. Barkley didn't get to the movies much. The last movie he'd seen was **Jurassic Bark**, way back when he was a pup.

KITTY DECLAW:

• Cat from Catifornia.
• Howlywood movie star.
• Likes milk.

Kitty DeClaw was an action-movie megastar. A total **glamourpuss**. A cat who'd moved out to Dogtown from Catifornia to make it **big** in Howlywood.

And here she was in the fur, sitting on a lounge chair and **sipping** milk while an overworked ring-tailed lemur fanned her.

"Fan **faster**!" yelled Kitty. "And get me another saucer of milk while you're at it!"

MEOWY CHOWY
TAKE #3

While everyone was busy looking at Kitty, Barkley **spotted** something interesting. Something **shiny**. Something **PINK!**

66

You guessed it. He'd spotted a pink **electric scooter**–
just like the one they had chased through Dogtown.
And here it was, **parked** on the set of this Meowy
Chowy TV ad.

"Psst! Fang. Look, it's the scooter! We need to get closer.
Here, put this on so no one recognizes us." Barkley
passed Fang a **BIG** pineapple hat.

The pair **snuck** through the crowd to the pink scooter.

It was true that no one would recognize them in those hats, but Barkley didn't think about the attention two **giant pineapples** might draw. Luckily, everyone was too busy staring at Kitty DeClaw to notice the Underdogs checking out the scooter.

Hmmm

Everyone but Kitty herself!

"Paws off my scooter, **pineapple heads**," purred Kitty DeClaw, all eyes on her.

"Sorry, Ms. DeClaw," said Fang. "We were just **admiring** it. So, it's your scooter then, is it?"

"That's right. Mine," replied Kitty, smiling **smugly**.

"And do you ride it much?" asked Barkley.

"Sometimes," said Kitty.

"Like earlier today, near Westbark Bank?"

Kitty **narrowed** her eyes.

No. I've been hard at work filming this Meowy Chowy ad. Now, why are you asking me all these questions?

"U-Umm…" stuttered Barkley. "We're just big **fans**…"

"Yeah, **BIG** fans. **HUGE!** I don't suppose we could get a selfie with you?" said Fang.

Kitty DeClaw sighed and stroked her **necklace**. "Fine," she said.

Fang **winked** at Barkley and he made sure the scooter was in the shot. **SNAP!**

Now they had evidence of the **getaway vehicle**, they just needed to find out who drove it. And all paws **pointed** to Kitty.

CAT BURGLAR

But it didn't make sense. Why would a **movie star** also have a **secret** career as a cat burglar?

Fang and Barkley waved goodbye. "Thanks, Ms. DeClaw. Have a **lovely** day."

Kitty smiled **dazzlingly** at them...

Then she turned and **snapped** at the exhausted lemur, "I said **milk**! Get me more milk!"

"Coming, Ms. DeClaw!" said the lemur.

Fang and Barkley wandered on, **thinking** deeply.

"Something's **fishy**, and it's not the cat food..." Barkley frowned.

"Yes," agreed Fang quietly. "That cat's **hiding** something. But we need to **sniff out** more clues before we can accuse Kitty DeClaw of being the cat burglar."

CHAPTER 6

Things were **heating** up. The pink scooter was the first clue. But something was wrong. **VERY** wrong… Can you guess what it was?

Yes, you're correct! Fang and Barkley hadn't eaten. They needed **lunch**!

"I know this place that makes the **best** dog food," Barkley said, licking his lips.

"Hmmm. I don't exactly **love** dog food…" said Fang.

"What do cats have for lunch, then?" asked Barkley.

"Well," said Fang, "I often have a double scoop of **mice cream**."

"Yuck," said Barkley. "You're putting me off my **pup-corn**! Maybe try this instead…" He handed her a can of something.

"Mrs. McTavish's Eel and Tentacle Soup? Bleerk!" Fang **scrunched** up her face.

"They were giving it away for free…" protested Barkley.

"I'm not **surprised**. And I'm not so hungry now, either," said Fang. "So, how long have you been an Underdog Detective, Barkley?"

"In dog years or cat years?" asked Barkley. "Either way, too long! I've been an Underdog since we were the **WONDERDOGS.**"

Fang looked **puzzled**. "The Wonderdogs?"

"Yeah. We lost the **W** and the top of the **O** a few years back. We never did work out who took them…" mused Barkley.

"I **see**," said Fang. She didn't see.

"So," said Barkley, "we don't have too many clues. Just a **pink scooter** and some **wet pawprints**."

Fang tapped her claws. "The wet pawprints just don't make sense. Cats **hate** water! But if they're not the cat burglar's pawprints, then whose are they?"

"No idea," mumbled Barkley.

"A **no-eye** deer? How could a deer with **NO EYES** even see the sardines in the first place?" Fang was confused.

Barkley shook his head. "Look, this scooter is the best clue we have. I say we have a little **snoop** around Kitty DeClaw's house."

So, the pair got on the bus and headed up to the Howlywood Hills, where all the **movie stars** had their **fancy** mansions.

"Now, part of being an Underdog is **snooping**," Barkley explained as they got to the front gates of Kitty DeClaw's **luxury** home. "Are you ready to do some snooping?"

But Fang had already climbed over the top of the **big** iron gate.

"Yeah. That's good. Now **sneak** around and see what you can see. I'll follow you in a moment..." Barkley looked up at the **high** gate. Climbing had never really been his strong point...

Meanwhile, Fang began snooping–treading as softly as a cat, which makes sense because **SHE IS A CAT!**

She **tiptoed** silently through the garden, then she was suddenly startled by a loud "**Pssst**!"

Fang looked back to see Barkley **stuck** halfway up the gate.

"Do you need a little help, Barkley?" asked Fang.

"No, I'm doing fine," panted Barkley. "I just wanted to say the secret to snooping is good **camouflage**. You have to **blend in** with your surroundings."

"Okay," said Fang, putting a potted plant on her head. "How's this?"

"Much better." Barkley gave her a thumbs-up. Well, more like a **claw-up**, because dogs don't really have thumbs.

At that **exact** moment, the front door opened.

Out stepped a **slinky** figure.

Can I help you?

"Oh, hello there, Ms. DeClaw," said Barkley. The way he said it, you'd think it was perfectly **normal** to be hanging on a **security gate** while your partner had a **potted plant** on their head.

But it wasn't Kitty DeClaw—it wasn't even a cat.
It was just that **lemur** again.

"Oh, sorry, I thought you were Ms. DeClaw," said Fang.

"Ms. DeClaw isn't in right now," explained the lemur.
"Do you mind telling me why you're wearing a potted
plant, and why you're **hanging** on Ms. DeClaw's gate?"

Barkley squared his shoulders and tried to look **professional**. As professional as anyone **clinging** to a gate can look, anyway. "We're detectives. We were hoping to ask her a few questions." Barkley showed the lemur his **card**. "You don't happen to know where we can find her, do you?"

The lemur **glanced** at Barkley's card, then back at the detectives. "Sure. She's on her way to the Howlton Hotel for the auction of the **Hope Diamond Collar**. She just **LOVES** diamonds."

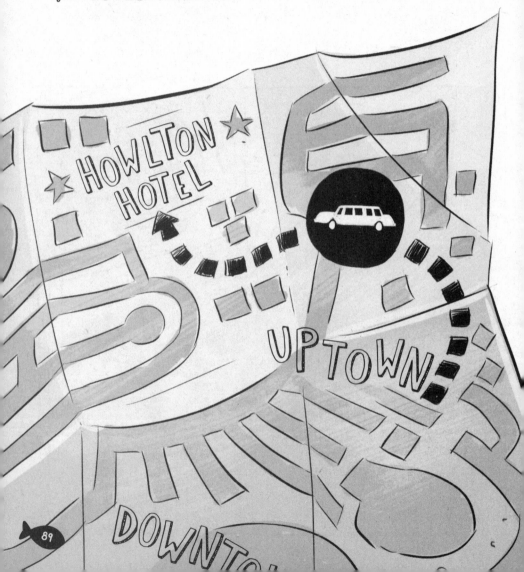

Interesting . . . thought Fang.
"And what's your name, miss?"
she asked.

"Rita Ringis," said the lemur
with an **exhausted** smile.
"I'm Ms. DeClaw's **stunt double**."

RITA RINGIS:
• Ring-tailed lemur.
• Personal assistant
  and stunt lemur.

CHAPTER 7

Back at the Underdog Detective Agency, the **fumes** of Mrs. McTavish's baked bean and beetroot soup were **wafting** through the floorboards.

Barkley was updating Carl and Dr. Spots on everything he and Fang had found out...which wasn't all that much.

"We have to get to this **auction** at the Howlton Hotel and keep a really close eye on Kitty," said Barkley. "And you know what that means…"

"You two need to go undercover!" replied Dr. Spots.

"Exactly," grinned Fang. "They don't call us **UNDERDOGS** for nothing!"

The Underdogs **cheered** and gave each other high fives. Or, to be exact, high fours. Like I said, dogs don't have thumbs.

"The only way a couple of **fleabags** like you and Fang can blend in with all those fancy rich folks is with some great **disguises**. And, lucky for you, I've been working on just the thing..." Dr. Spots opened up a cupboard crammed full of **wonderful gadgets** and disguises.

"Cool!" said Fang, grabbing an **astronaut** suit.

Barkley growled. "We're trying to blend in, not take a walk on the **moon**!" He grabbed a **top hat** and a fancy black suit jacket for himself.

"Is this better?" asked Fang, picking up an **elaborate headdress** with apples, oranges, bananas, and grapes piled high on top.

"That's not a disguise, Fang," Spots said. "Those are my **groceries**."

Dr. Spots handed Fang another top hat and suit jacket. Fang put it on. She and Barkley actually looked **pretty fancy**.

"Not bad," said Dr. Spots, looking them up and down. "Now just remember, Kitty DeClaw is a **VIP. A Very Important Pussycat**. It's going to be hard to get close to her, even looking this fancy!"

Barkley **winked** at Fang. Looking this good, **anything** was possible.

WINK!

The Howlton Hotel was buzzing with folks in their fine fur coats. There were **dazzling** dogs, **fancy** ferrets, and **swanky** squirrels all arriving in limousines. Someone was even arriving by helicopter!

"Oh drat!" said Barkley. "The Top Dogs are here."

"Are they **really** detectives?" asked Fang. "They look like movie stars!"

"Don't tell them that," groaned Barkley. "They already think they're the best thing since **canned dog food**. They even have their own **TV show**—*Real Detectives of Dogtown.*"

The Top Dogs stopped and **posed** for the cameras.

One reporter pushed a microphone toward the **stylish** dogs. "Top Dogs! What are you doing here?"

"We're here to make sure the Hope Diamond Collar doesn't go walkies," **snickered** the siblings.

Everyone laughed. Everyone **except** Barkley. "I bet they start talking about how great they are," he whispered, **rolling** his eyes.

"And did we mention, we're the **greatest**?" said the Top Dogs.

"Come on, let's get in there," said Fang.

FLASH!

FLASH!

Fang and Barkley followed the Top Dogs toward the ballroom. The bulldog security guard **smiled** and waved the **celebrity** detectives through.

"It looks pretty easy to get in…" whispered Barkley, but they were soon **blocked** by the bulldog's mean **scowl**.

"Your names?" barked the security bulldog, looking at his list.

"Umm, we're not on the list **exactly**…"

"No name, no entry!"

"But…"

"No exceptions!" **growled** the security bulldog. "Now scram!"

Fang's heart **skipped** a beat. If they didn't get in, they'd never **catch** the cat burglar. With some **quick** thinking, Fang put on her **fanciest** voice.

Don't you recognize me? I'm the Royal Countess Shablar Blar Blar Blar Blar Blar.

The door dog **checked** his list. He checked it again. He looked confused. "I'm sorry, Countess. I don't seem to have you on the list…"

"There's a very good reason for that… I'm traveling **in-cog-nito**," replied Fang sternly.

"Oh, why didn't you say! In that case, let me add your name to the list," **stammered** the bulldog. "How do I spell Shablar…"

B-L-A-R, B-L-A-R, B-L-A-R, B-L-A-R, B-L-A-R. It's French.

"Of course. Please come in, Countess Shablar Blar Blar Blar Blar Blar." He looked at Barkley. "And **you** must be Count Shablar Blar Blar Blar Blar Blar Blar?"

"No, my name is Sir Nigel Shrubbington-Bottomly-Smitty."

"Sir Nigel Shrubbington-Bottomly-Smitty," said the bulldog, checking his **clipboard**. "Oh yes, there you are. Welcome, Sir Nigel Shrubbington-Bottomly-Smitty."

As they climbed the stairs to the entrance, Fang gave Barkley a smile. "**Amazing**! How did you do that?"

"Easy—I **read** it on his clipboard. When you've been an Underdog for as long as me, you have a few **tricks** up your sleeve."

Fang and Barkley took a **deep breath**, then stepped inside the ballroom. It had **marble** floors, **golden** statues and waiters handing out **crystal** water bowls and tiny little dog bones. It sure was fancy. **REALLY FANCY!**

But Fang wasn't here to be impressed, she was here to **spy** on Kitty DeClaw... but where was she?

Fang didn't need to **wonder** very long. At that moment, the detectives heard the security bulldog behind them **bark**...

Ms. DeClaw! How wonderful to see you! Please, please come in!

CHAPTER 8

Fang quickly **spun** around. It was Kitty all right, and she was **dripping** in diamonds.

With the cameras **flashing** everywhere, this was Fang and Barkley's chance to hide. They stepped behind a golden statue of a peeing pug dog and **watched** as Kitty moved into the ballroom.

"Hello, Ms. DeClaw!" said a beagle, **slobbering** on Kitty's pristine paw.

"So **wonderful** you're here. Will you be **bidding** on the Hope Diamond Collar?" asked a gopher in a bow tie.

"Well, I should certainly like it to come home with me!" purred Kitty. Everyone **laughed**. Well, everyone except Fang and Barkley.

The auctioneer entered the room carrying the **biggest diamond** Fang had ever seen. The light danced off it like a disco ball. The crowd **gasped**. Barkley took a step closer. Fang's eyes narrowed.

"The Hope Diamond Collar!" shouted the auctioneer. "The most **beautiful** and most **expensive** collar in the world! The auction will begin in one hour."

Fang looked for the Top Dogs—surely they would be keeping a close eye on the collar. She **scanned** the room and saw them standing in a circle of fancy guests, **chowing down** on party snacks.

They weren't watching the collar at all! They were still talking about how **great** they were!

We're definitely the greatest detectives in Dogtown.

Did I mention we have a helicopter with our names on it?

Barkley was right about those dogs—they sure liked to **show off**.

In the **distraction**, the Underdogs had taken their eyes off Kitty. Where was she? Fang and Barkley searched the room…

She was there just a **moment** ago!

but she was **gone**!

Fang **sniffed** the air, but all the perfume made it impossible to catch a cat's **scent**.

AHHHCHOOOOO!

Fang would have to rely on her **super** cat eyes to scan the crowd.
But wait… what was that? A swish of a black-and-white tail sneaking through the staff door. **Kitty**!

STAFF ONLY

Fang and Barkley put their paws to the floor and **darted** through the crowd.

CRASH! Barkley ran right into a waiter carrying a tower of glasses!

Don't let that cat get away!

Fang pushed open the kitchen door just as Kitty's tail **disappeared** into the staff elevator.

This made no sense! The Hope Diamond Collar was in the **ballroom**, along with all the guests. The only thing upstairs would be hotel rooms, and they'd be **empty**!

That cat's going to miss the auction! It's the whole reason she's here, thought Fang.

UNLESS . . .

THAT'S IT! She wasn't after the Hope Diamond Collar at all! She was going to rob the rooms while everyone was at the auction! **GENIUS!**

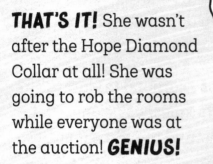

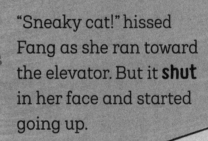

"Sneaky cat!" hissed Fang as she ran toward the elevator. But it **shut** in her face and started going up.

SLAM!

Fang **spun** around. "There's more than one way to follow that cat. I'll climb the **laundry chute**!"

Fang **leaped** into the laundry chute and **scampered** up, climbing over old socks and even older underpants … but she was too slow. On every floor, doors were **wide open**. The rooms were **ransacked**.

"The only way is up! She's going to the **penthouse!**" exclaimed Fang as she **raced** to the top floor.

The door to the penthouse was **open**. There was no way out. The cat burglar had to be inside. This was Fang's **big chance**.

The door **creaked** and Fang froze, then she moved silently into the room. Her cat eyes could see **perfectly** in the dark.

"This is Detective Fang. There's no escape!" called Fang in her best detective voice.

In the dark, Fang saw a **masked** figure. Its paws were up.

"Okay, good. Keep your **paws** where I can see them!" warned Fang.

Suddenly, the figure **leaped** across the room and out onto the balcony!

"STOP!" yelled Fang. She jumped toward the cat burglar, but the **sneaky** thief was too quick.

Just then, a loud **roar** came from the sky...

Fang looked up.

Bright lights. **Loud** whirring.

It was a **helicopter**!

It was the Top Dogs' helicopter, but the Top Dogs weren't flying it—the **UNDERDOGS** were.

"**Ha**!" laughed the cat burglar. She took one look at the **chopper** and **jumped** over the balcony railing to the street far below, holding a large sack of **stolen jewels**.

WOW!

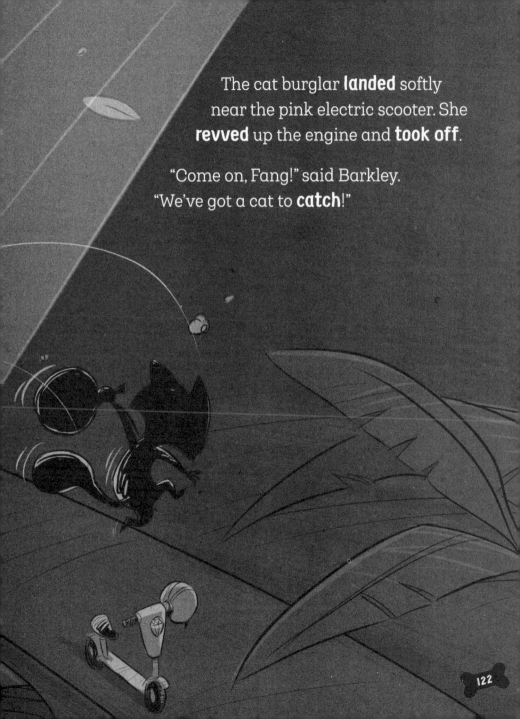

The cat burglar **landed** softly
near the pink electric scooter. She
revved up the engine and **took off**.

"Come on, Fang!" said Barkley.
"We've got a cat to **catch**!"

CHAPTER 9

"Follow that cat!" yelled Fang as she **leaped** from the balcony into the waiting chopper.

"You got it!" said Barkley. "We're not losing her this time!"

The pink scooter **swerved** and **zipped** through the streets of Dogtown. As fast as the scooter was, though, the helicopter was faster.

"How did you get the Top Dogs' helicopter?" yelled Fang to Carl as he **steered** the chopper over buildings.

"They thought I was the **parking valet**!" said Carl with a **smile**.

The scooter was headed toward the **Howlywood Hills**—toward Kitty DeClaw's mansion.

Sure enough, the scooter pulled into the driveway of Kitty's place. The rider **jumped** off, and ran through the front door.

"Okay, Fang. Time to **crack this case**," said Barkley. "Carl, get us as low as you can so we can jump out."

"Okey-dokey!" Carl replied. "And then I'll need to find someplace to land this **whirlybird**!"

Carl **hovered** as low as he could go, but because of all the trees in Kitty's garden, he was still pretty **high** up. "That's as close as I can get."

Fang knew just what to do. After all, she was a cat.

A jumping, climbing, **FEARLESS CAT.**

She took a **mighty** leap out of the helicopter and scrambled right down the trunk of a palm tree, landing on her feet. Cats **always** land on their feet.

"Yesss!" barked Barkley, Carl, and Dr. Spots, **punching** their **paws** in the air. Unfortunately, in that split second when his paws were off the wheel, Carl lost **control** of the helicopter...

Right into Kitty DeClaw's **swimming pool**.

Luckily, the Underdogs **bobbed** to the surface a few seconds later.

"Don't worry about us. Dogs can **swim**. Unlike cats... and helicopters!" said Dr. Spots, looking over at the **submerged** helicopter. "Now go find that cat burglar!"

Fang and Barkley **raced** off. Barkley ran inside, where a black-and-white tail was **disappearing** up the marble staircase.

He raced up the stairs, but marble + wet paws = **SPLAT!**

SPLAT!

By the time he made it to the upstairs bedroom, the cat burglar was **nowhere** to be found.

SPLAT!

Fang **booked** it to the back of the property. If the cat burglar made a **dash** out the back door, Fang would be on her in a flash. Suddenly, Fang's ears pricked up. **Footsteps!** Soft, muffled footsteps... on the roof! She looked up and saw a **shadowy** figure outlined against the full moon. **THE CAT BURGLAR!**

"Stop right there!" Fang took a running jump. She **soared** into the air, **catching** a tree branch, and **swung** onto the tiled roof of Kitty's mansion. The cat burglar crouched, ready to make her own **giant leap** to freedom.

But Fang was too fast.

HISS!

A fierce **caterwauling** filled the air as Fang and the cat burglar **rolled** down the roof.

SCRATCH!

BANG!

Barkley looked out the bedroom window just in time to see Fang and the cat burglar **plummet** to the ground.

"**FANG!**" shouted Barkley. He looked down below.

He expected the **worst**, but what did he see? Fang had landed on her **feet**. Right on **top** of the cat burglar.

Oh no! Oh no!

CHAPTER 10

Barkley **rushed** outside to where Fang and the cat burglar were nursing their **sore** tails.

"So it was you all along, Kitty DeClaw," said Fang as the **woozy** cat burglar started to wake up.

Barkley's eyes widened.

FURBALLS! That's not Kitty DeClaw!

At the gates, a **limousine** had just arrived. The driver raced around to open the door… and Kitty DeClaw stepped out! Glistening around her neck was the **Hope Diamond Collar.**

"But… but… you're **KITTY DECLAW!**" said Fang.

"The **one** and **only**," purred Kitty.

Then who's this?

"Only one way to find out," said Fang, as she pulled off the suspect's scooter **helmet**.

It wasn't a **cat**.

It was a **LEMUR!**

SHOONK!

The Underdogs gasped. "**Rita Ringis**! No way!"

"Yes way!" Rita cried out. "Who else could have made all those **daring** jumps but a ring-tailed lemur?"

Kitty looked like she might **faint**.

"But Rita ... why?" asked Fang.

"I do all the **stunts** while Kitty gets all the **credit** ... and all the **diamonds**!" Rita turned to Kitty. "I get you all those saucers of milk, and you **_NEVER SAY THANK YOU!_**"

Kitty looked surprised, and a bit **embarrassed**. "This is **outrageous**! And after all I've done for you!"

"Is it true you **never** say thank you?" asked Fang.

"You know how cats can be," said Kitty weakly.

Fang just shook her head.

Barkley spoke up. "**Leaping lemurs**! I get the diamonds, but why does a lemur steal a whole bunch of **sardines**?"

"I think I know why," Fang said. "You see, Rita wanted to make it look like Kitty was the cat burglar. She knew no one would suspect a **lemur** of stealing sardines… they're **vegetarian**! But cats, we just love sardines!"

"That explains the **puddly** footprints," mused Barkley. "Lemurs are happy to wade through water."

"I wasn't trying to **hurt** anyone!" cried Rita.

CASE NOTES
Kitty: ??
* Loves sardines
* Hates water
* Can jump high!

CAT BURGLAR

"I was just trying to **teach** Kitty a lesson. She's always so rude!"

Kitty took a breath. "I'm sorry, Rita. I guess I have been a total **glamourpuss**. Maybe we can both do something to clean up the mess we've made?"

Rita looked **skeptical**. "Like what?"

The Underdogs looked at each other. "We've got **just** the idea!"

With a little help from the Underdogs, Rita returned all the **jewels** back to the hotel guests.

Then she went **downtown** and paid the bank a visit. She gave them back all their money, and **promised** to never set foot in the bank again.

There was only one thing she couldn't return...
SARDINES! Too stinky. So she made it up to Max Pelicano by using her high-wire skills to **wash** every single **window** at the fish market.

There were **1,200** windows in total... but luckily she had a little help from a friend.

The Underdogs had **cracked** the **case** and set things right.

"I guess we can all go home and take a well-earned break. I'm going to spend a bit of time with my **favorite** chew toy…" said Barkley.

Fang nodded. "**CASE CLOSED!**"

But just at that moment, a **text** came through from Carl.

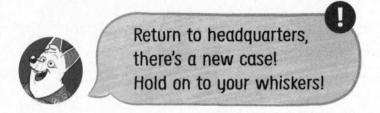

Return to headquarters,
there's a new case!
Hold on to your whiskers!

Barkley looked at Fang. "In a town that's gone
to the **dogs**, we sure need a **cat** like you."

Go, team!

THE END

DO **YOU** HAVE WHAT IT TAKES TO BE AN **UNDERDOG** DETECTIVE?

SEARCH & FIND

A good detective can find hidden evidence. Can you find these ten words in the below grid?

CARL DISGUISE CHASE GADGET TAIL
SOLVED DOGTOWN UNDERCOVER CRIME DIAMOND

```
B M G E J T L H N F E I U A J
R C G M R Q R M G S Q W U R P
K M N I Z M A A I C H A S E Q
G E O R P F C U E S Q G N J C
T R V C K L G J O V R Y L K G
T O E U B S D L M D D Z J Y K
J B E V I C V A N W O T G O D
F D U D O E X O T O V Y Z N T
L F J R D C M M B C K K V J W
G Y M E O A R F Y F Q G I W H
I A S P I Z Z E N U A I L J S
A U D D Z Y K P D Z A C S T X
J T L G P T B H F N V X X A B
X O S T E F L Q R F U S Q I J
G H Q H W T Y C S J V P N L B
```

WORD SCRAMBLE

A good detective uses clues to solve a mystery. Can you complete the below sentence by unscrambling the ten clues?

Now that Fang is part of the team, she and the Underdogs are:

_ _ _ _ / _ _ _ _ _ _ _ _ / _ _ _ _ _ _ _ !

YIEBCLC	◯ _ _ _ _ _ ◯
ORSTPSD	_ _ ◯ _ _ _ ◯ _
AFGN	◯ _ _ _
SSENDIRA	_ _ ◯ _ ◯ _ ◯ _
SGUNOERDD	_ ◯ _ _ _ ◯ _ _ ◯
GCAEOFLAUM	_ _ _ _ _ ◯ _ _ _ _
GRUBLRA	_ ◯ _ _ _ _ _
NWTRSPPAI	_ _ _ _ _ ◯ _ _ _ _
VTITDECEE	_ ◯ _ _ _ _ _ ◯ ◯
LEBAYKR	_ _ ◯ _ _ _ _

A good detective knows when something is out of place. Can you find the ten differences between these two pictures?

ANSWER KEY 🐾

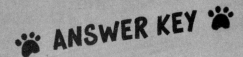

So how did you do?

WORD SCRAMBLE

Bicycle, Dr Spots,
Fang, Sardines,
Underdogs,
Camouflage,
Burglar, Pawprints,
Detective, Barkley.

Answer to the clues:
BEST FRIENDS *FUR*EVER!

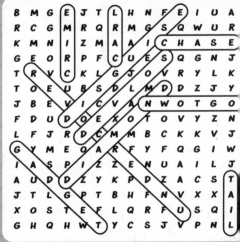

SPOT THE DIFFERENCE

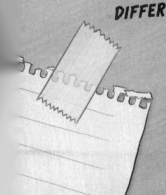

IF YOU HAVE A PROBLEM YOU JUST CAN'T SOLVE, CALL*

The UNDER DOGS

1-800-UNDERDOGS

BARKLEY

DR. SPOTS

FANG

CARL

*If you speak to Carl, hang up and call back until someone else answers.

CRIME IS ON THE RISE IN DOGTOWN, AND IT'S ALL THANKS TO AN ART FORGER!

They've stolen one of Puplo Picasso's masterpieces out of a museum and swapped it with a fake. Such a big case would normally go to the Top Dog detectives, but they're out of town on vacation . . .

So it's time to call in the Underdogs! And they are determined to catch the culprit and prove they are the best sleuths in town. Can Fang, Barkley, and the others solve the case before the thief strikes again or the Top Dogs return from their trip?

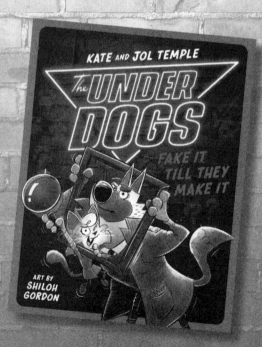